Thanks to
Anne Brouillard

Text and illustrations © 1996, l'école des loisirs, Paris

First U.S. edition, 2000

Originally published in French by Pastel, Paris.

For information address Hyperion Books for Children, 114 Fifth Avenue, New York, New York 10011-5690.

1 3 5 7 9 10 8 6 4 2

Printed in Hong Kong.

Library of Congress Cataloging-in-Publication Data

Crowther, Kitty.

Jack and Jim / by Kitty Crowther.

p. cm.

Summary: Jack the blackbird and Jim the seagull become friends, but Jack is sad that
the other seagulls do not seem to like him.

ISBN: 0-7868-0614-1 (trade) - ISBN 0-7868-2527-8 (lib.)

[1. Birds-Fiction. 2. Friendship-Fiction. 3. Prejudices-Fiction.] I Title.

PZ7.C88792 Jac 2000

[E]-dc21

00-039724

Visit www.hyperionchildrensbooks.com

Jack & Jim

Kitty Crowther

HYPERION BOOKS FOR CHILDREN
NEW YORK

Jack had always dreamed of seeing the world. Most of all, he longed to fly over the sea, so blue and wide.

So one sunny day, he decided to cross the forest.

And then the hills.

On the other side of the hills, he found the sea.

Jack was preparing to take off and soar out over the gleaming water when he noticed something sticking up from behind a rock.

"Whose feet are these?" he wondered out loud.

"How do you do?" said a seagull.
"My name is Jim."

"I'm Jack," said Jack shyly.
"Are you a real sea bird?"

Jim laughed. "Of course!
Would you like to see
where I live?"

Jack had never been so excited!

He and Jim flew together all day.

At the end of the day, they landed, exhausted, on a little island and talked and talked as the sun fell into the ocean and the stars began to twinkle in the sky.

Very early in the morning, Jim sneaked away to gather some supplies. When he returned, Jack was still fast asleep.

They shared a breakfast of tea and fish. Jack ate one fish and decided he preferred tea.

After breakfast, they flew to Jim's village.

What an amazing place! Seagulls hustled and bustled about. So different from the forest, thought Jack.

After they explored the town for a while, a strange feeling came over Jack. "Why is everyone staring at me, Jim?"

"It must be the first time they've ever seen a blackbird," said Jim. "I guess they're curious about you."

Still, Jack seemed unsure. Jim thought for a moment. Then he said, "Why don't I show you my place?"

"Here it is! My very own home—I built it myself."
Jim beamed with pride.

"At night, you can hear the waves. It's just like being in a boat."

Inside, they sat and talked, each with a cup of hot cocoa.

They settled down for the night, and Jim fell asleep right away.

But Jack was wide-awake. He was thinking about what a wonderful day he had had with his new friend.

It wasn't until the sun began to peek up over the water that he fell asleep . . . smiling.

The next morning, Jack and Jim ventured
back into the village. The port was teeming
with activity.

"Who's that funny bird?" asked
old Captain Seagull.

"His name is Jack. He's a blackbird,"
answered Jim. "He lives in the forest
on the other side of the sea."

"Jack is my friend."

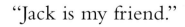

But the seagulls didn't like the
blackbird.

"I'd better go back home," said Jack quietly.
"No, you won't!" Jim was furious. "If that's the
way things are, we won't come to the village
anymore!"

And he led his friend away.

The next day they went fishing. Jim tried to cheer his friend up. "Don't worry, Jack. They'll come around soon."
But Jack was still sad.

"And if they don't, I'll come to your place!" Jim said.

Jack smiled. Jim truly was his friend.

The next day, Jim took Jack to visit a nearby forest of fir trees.

Jack was thrilled to feel so at home. He spent the day teaching Jim all about the forest.

Jack was happy that Jim liked his home, too.

Late that afternoon, back at Jim's house, Jack discovered a chest filled with books.
"I found it washed up on the beach," explained Jim.

"What luck!" Jack was delighted.
"Have you read any of them yet?"
"What?" asked Jim, puzzled. "I can't read . . . No one in the village can."

"In the forest," announced Jack, "everybody reads."

That night, Jack read Jim his first story.

The two friends had no idea that someone was secretly listening.

Later, Norbert told his mother about Jack's stories.

"Perhaps this blackbird isn't so bad after all," said Norbert's mother. "Why don't we go and visit him?"

She told her friends at the market about the stories and about her visit.

Martha and Melissa decided to go and meet Jack for themselves.

That evening, as Jack read to Jim, a group of seagulls quietly
approached the little wooden house. Jack had a fine, clear voice.

Every day new visitors came bringing gifts of flowers, fresh bread, and marmalade. Everyone wanted to meet Jack!

Now the seagulls greeted Jack with a big smile when they saw him in the village. That made Jack happy.

From then on he read funny stories that made Jim laugh.

And all his new friends laughed, too!

The End.